Laurie Parker

Mad For MAROON

Written and Illustrated by
LAURIE PARKER

For the Gray Family:
Ted, Paula, Joey and Elizabeth

Acknowledgment:

BIG thanks to Cyndi Clark for being the true friend
and gifted graphic artist that you are!

Thanks also to Carolyn Abadie for your friendship and support!

Production by Cyndi Clark.
Printed and bound in South Korea by Pacifica Communications.

9 8 7 6 5 4 3 2

I'm happy it's Saturday. This is the day.
We're going to Starkville to see the DAWGS play!
We carry our cowbells. We wear our maroon.
We show bulldog spirit the whole afternoon.

We pull into town with a long line of fans
Who come by the carload in RVs and vans.
With paw-printed windows, they drive one by one
To MSU's campus for football and fun.

The fields and the parking lots there are all strewn
With tailgating folks who are MAD for MAROON.
There's good food and fellowship prior to each game
And friends greet each other: "I'm so glad you came!"
They fire up their grills and mmm, boy—it smells great!
Barbecue! Chicken! I hardly can wait!

After partaking of fine cooked-out treats,
We head toward Scott Field with our stadium seats.
The stands fill up quickly. The game will start soon.
The crowd is a sea of the color maroon.
I see maroon caps, maroon cups, maroon vests
And college boys baring maroon-painted chests.

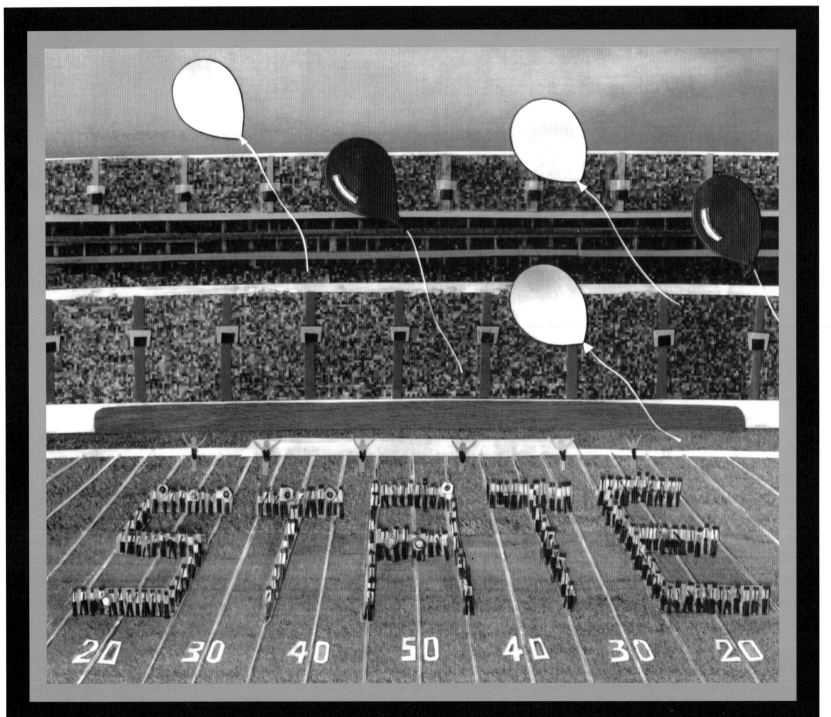

The pre-game festivities start with the band.
They're famous, maroon, and their show is just grand!
Trumpets and tubas and clear clarinets...
Drummers and flag girls and pert majorettes...
They march on the field and get into position.
They spell the word **STATE**. It's a long-held tradition.

The American Flag at Scott Field proudly flies.
With MSU caps to our hearts, we all rise.
Women and men, black and white, old and young—
We stand as our National Anthem is sung.
After the reverent pause for its singing
A loud cheer erupts and the cowbells start ringing!

The fanfare continues. I like the routine
When Bully, our mascot, appears on the scene.
He rides on his doghouse. He's really a hoot!
He's "bad to the bone," and yet cuddly and cute.

The MSU players come running out fast
As "Hail State," our fight song, is played at full blast.
We hoot and we holler. We clap to the tune.
We're here for our team and we're MAD for MAROON!

It's kickoff time finally. The game's underway.
I follow the action through play after play.
First downs and field goals and scrambles and fumbles...
Blitzes and blocking and tackles and tumbles...
Rushing and options and passes and punts—
I get to see some of the plays more than once
Thanks to the Jumbotron replays of stunts.

Our cheerleaders chant, "Got some DAWGS up in here!"
I join in and bark out, "Woof! Woof!" with that cheer.

A touchdown for State makes the crowd really roar.
I jump up and down and rejoice when we score.

Yes, I back the Bulldogs. I'm sure you can tell.
I shake my maroon and white pompom and yell.
And whether we win or we lose in the end
I'll have a good time at each game I attend.
And when the game's over, and we're heading out
I turn and I wave toward the sidelines and shout...

"...BYE FOR NOW, BULLY!
I'LL SEE YA REAL SOON!"

'Cause I love to come here!

I'm

MAD for MAROON!

If you didn't smile big while reading all this
Then you must be someone who roots for _ _ _   _ _ _ _.

THE
END